**Parents and Caregivers,**

Stone Arch Readers are designed to provide enjoyable reading experiences, as well as opportunities to develop vocabulary, literacy skills, and comprehension. Here are a few ways to support your beginning reader:

- Talk with your child about the ideas addressed in the story.
- Discuss each illustration, mentioning the characters, where they are, and what they are doing.
- Read with expression, pointing to each word. You may want to read the whole story through and then revisit parts of the story to ensure that the meanings of words or phrases are understood.
- Talk about why the character did what he or she did and what your child would do in that situation.
- Help your child connect with characters and events in the story.

Remember, reading with your child should be fun, not forced. Each moment spent reading with your child is a priceless investment in his or her literacy life.

**Gail Saunders-Smith, Ph.D.**

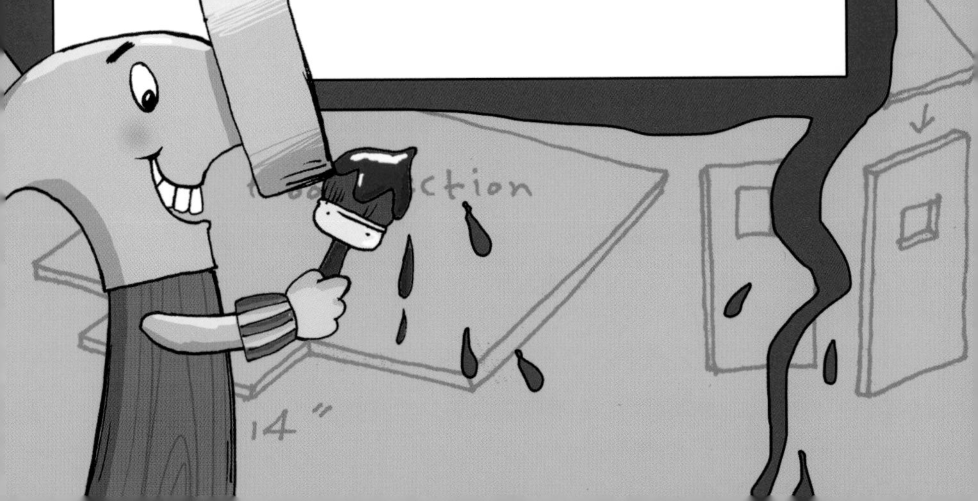

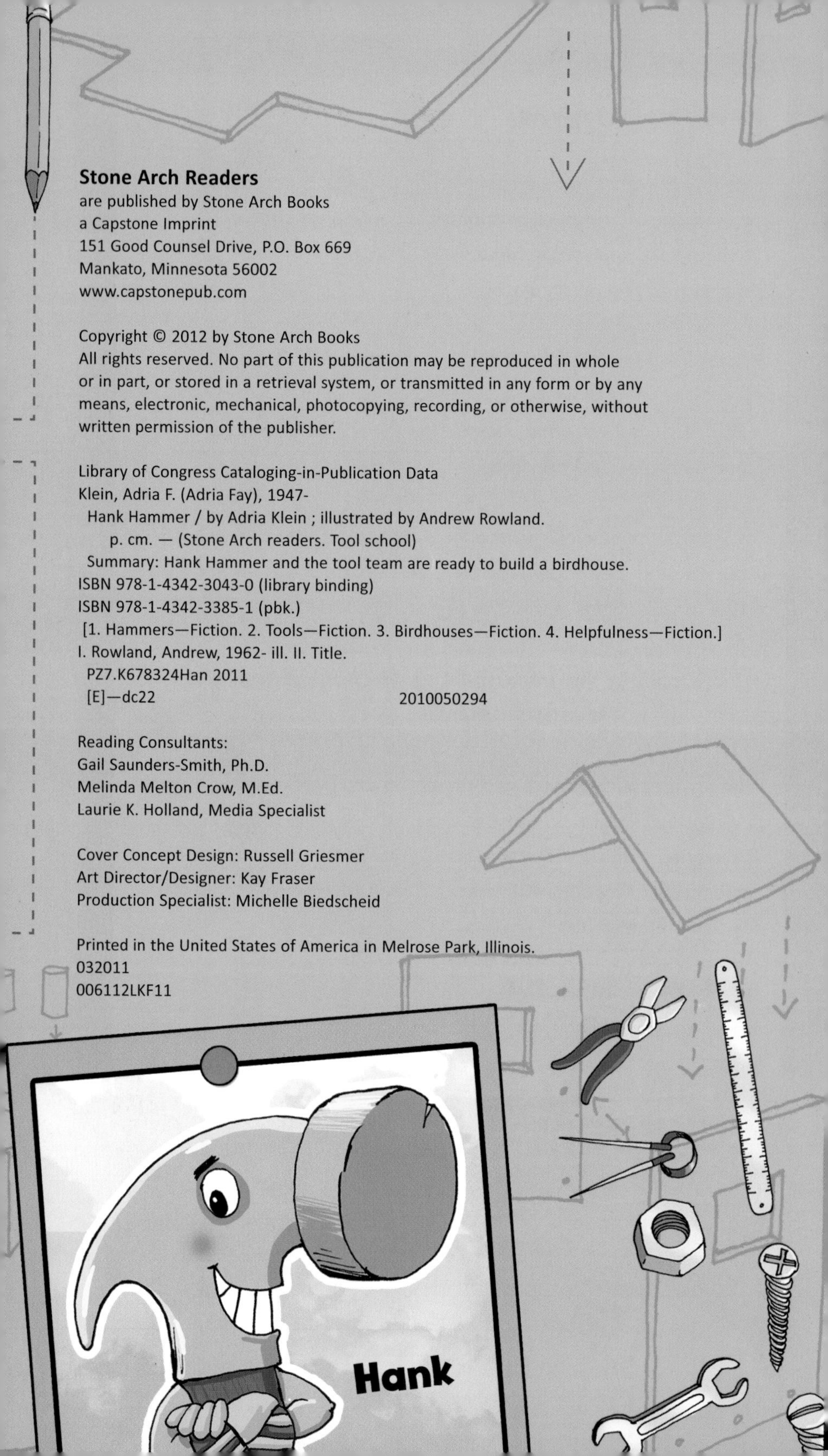


**Stone Arch Readers**
are published by Stone Arch Books
a Capstone Imprint
151 Good Counsel Drive, P.O. Box 669
Mankato, Minnesota 56002
www.capstonepub.com



Library of Congress Cataloging-in-Publication Data
Klein, Adria F. (Adria Fay), 1947-
Hank Hammer / by Adria Klein ; illustrated by Andrew Rowland.
p. cm. — (Stone Arch readers. Tool school)
Summary: Hank Hammer and the tool team are ready to build a birdhouse.
ISBN 978-1-4342-3043-0 (library binding)
ISBN 978-1-4342-3385-1 (pbk.)
[1. Hammers—Fiction. 2. Tools—Fiction. 3. Birdhouses—Fiction. 4. Helpfulness—Fiction.]
I. Rowland, Andrew, 1962- ill. II. Title.
PZ7.K678324Han 2011
[E]—dc22 2010050294

Reading Consultants:
Gail Saunders-Smith, Ph.D.
Melinda Melton Crow, M.Ed.
Laurie K. Holland, Media Specialist

Cover Concept Design: Russell Griesmer
Art Director/Designer: Kay Fraser
Production Specialist: Michelle Biedscheid

Printed in the United States of America in Melrose Park, Illinois.
032011
006112LKF11

# Hank Hammer

by Adria Klein    illustrated by Andy Rowland

MEET THE
TOOL
TEAM
Tia Tape Measure
Hank Hammer
5
4
3
2
1
floor section
8 x 14"

Sammy Saw
Sophie Screwdriver
8 x 14"

Today is the big contest. Hank is very excited! He jumps out of bed.

He brushes his teeth and gets ready.

“Have a fun day,” his mom says.
“Good luck at the contest.”

“Thanks, Mom,” Hank says as he rushes out the door.

“Hi, everyone! Are you ready for the big contest?” asks Hank.

"We're ready!" they yell.

"I have the wood," says Sammy.

"I have the nails," says Tia.

"I have the red paint and the blue paint," says Sophie.

"And I have the plans," says Hank.

"We are going to build the best birdhouse!" says Sammy.

"It's time to start," says Sophie.

"What do we do?" asks Tia.

"Just follow my plan," says Hank. "I have everything mapped out right here."

“First, we measure everything,” says Hank.

"That's my job," says Tia.

"Great!" says Hank.

"Next, we cut the wood,"
says Hank.

"That's my job," says Sammy.

"Great!" says Hank.

“Then, we put the house together,” says Hank.

"I'll hold the nails. You can pound them in," says Sophie.

"Great!" says Hank.

“Now we paint it,” says Hank.

"We can all do that," says Sophie.

"Great!" says Hank.

The birdhouse is done. The tool team sets it on the table next to the other ones.

“It’s perfect,” says Hank.

"I think we built the best one,"
says Sammy.

"And we did it together," says Tia.

"I have one more thing to add," says Hank.

"Now it's perfect," says Sammy.

contest

measure

build

birdhouse

follow

together

Total Word Count: 241